mini Look and Find

Disney · PIXAR

TOY STORY 2

Written by Lynn Roberts
Illustrated by Animagination, Inc., and the Disney Storybook Artists

© Disney Enterprises, Inc./Pixar
Original Toy Story Elements © Disney Enterprises, Inc. All rights reserved.
Fire Truck by Little Tikes® Little Tikes Toys © The Little Tikes Company
Toddle Tots® by Little Tikes® Little Tikes Toys © The Little Tikes Company
Little Tikes Toys © The Little Tikes Company

This publication may not be reproduced in whole or in part by any means whatsoever without
written permission from the copyright owners. Permission is never granted for commercial purposes.

Published by Louis Weber, C.E.O., Publications International, Ltd.
7373 North Cicero Avenue, Lincolnwood, Illinois 60712
Ground Floor, 59 Gloucester Place, London W1U 8JJ

Customer Service: 1-800-595-8484 or customer_service@pilbooks.com

www.pilbooks.com

p i kids is a registered trademark of Publications International, Ltd.
Mini Look and Find is a trademark of Publications International, Ltd.
Look and Find is a registered trademark of Publications International, Ltd.,
in the United States and in Canada.

8 7 6 5 4 3 2 1

Manufactured in China.

ISBN-13: 978-1-60553-553-1
ISBN-10: 1-60553-553-2

pi kids ® **publications international, ltd.**

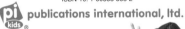

D1416096

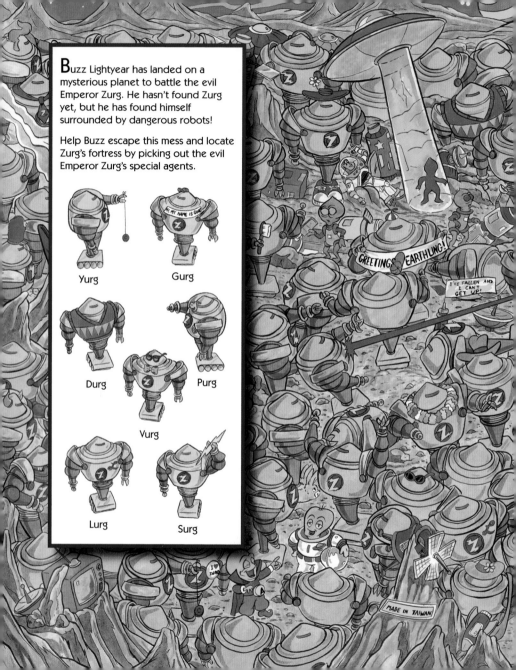

Buzz Lightyear has landed on a mysterious planet to battle the evil Emperor Zurg. He hasn't found Zurg yet, but he has found himself surrounded by dangerous robots!

Help Buzz escape this mess and locate Zurg's fortress by picking out the evil Emperor Zurg's special agents.

Yurg

Gurg

Durg

Purg

Vurg

Lurg

Surg

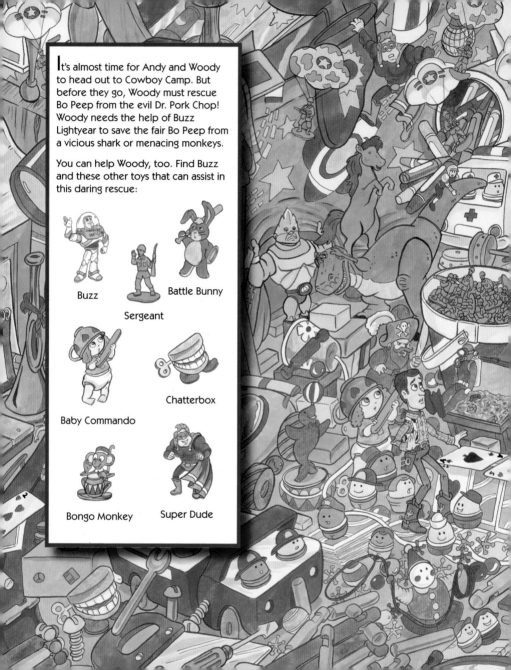

It's almost time for Andy and Woody to head out to Cowboy Camp. But before they go, Woody must rescue Bo Peep from the evil Dr. Pork Chop! Woody needs the help of Buzz Lightyear to save the fair Bo Peep from a vicious shark or menacing monkeys.

You can help Woody, too. Find Buzz and these other toys that can assist in this daring rescue:

Buzz

Sergeant

Battle Bunny

Baby Commando

Chatterbox

Bongo Monkey

Super Dude

Woody was left behind from Cowboy Camp, but now he has a chance to be a real cowboy. Woody must save Wheezy from being sold at the yard sale. With the help of the family dog, Buster, Woody makes the trip into the yard. But where's Wheezy?

Look through all this old junk to help Woody find Wheezy. While you're at it, find Woody, Buster, and some other fun treasures.

Woody

Lava Lamp

Wheezy

Bicentennial Teapot

This Record Album

Roller Skates

Buster

Woody has been captured from the yard sale by Al from Al's Toy Barn! Now Woody is far from Andy's room and all his old friends. But it turns out that Woody was a big TV star and everyone from *Woody's Roundup* treats him like a star cowboy!

Look around Al's apartment to find this Woody merchandise:

Woody Button

Cowboy Woody
Safety Scissors

Woody's Toothpaste

Roundup Pencil Box

Woody's
Fun Foam

Cowboy
Woody Soda

Woody's Roundup
Thermos

Andy's toys are on a mission to save Woody. They have to get to Al's Toy Barn, but first they must cross many lanes of the busiest traffic anyone has ever seen! It's risky business, but they're just the toys for the job!

As Buzz, Hamm, and Rex dodge traffic, look at all the crazy vehicles to find these fun things that seem a little too familiar:

Buzz Lightyear
Air Freshener

This Sign

This Cup Holder

This Dashboard
Ornament

HAMM

This License Plate

Funky Monkey
Fringe

There are so many toys and games inside Al's Toy Barn! Buzz, Rex, and Hamm have been searching for Woody among the shelves, but the only luck they've had has been finding a guidebook to defeating the evil Emperor Zurg for the Buzz Lightyear video game!

Look through the toys to find Buzz, Rex, Hamm, and these crazy characters they have met here:

Dirk Soldier

Rex

Buzz

Speedy Racer

Hamm

Rhonda Ragdoll

Evil Emperor Zurg

Al is taking Woody and the other Roundup collectibles to Japan to be put in a museum! Andy's toys need to rescue Woody from Al's suitcase before he gets loaded onto the plane. Some of the other Roundup toys help out because they don't want to go either.

You can help! Find Buzz, Woody, Jessie, Hamm, Rex, and Bullseye in this roller coaster ride of suitcases.

Buzz

Woody

Rex

Hamm

Bullseye

Jessie

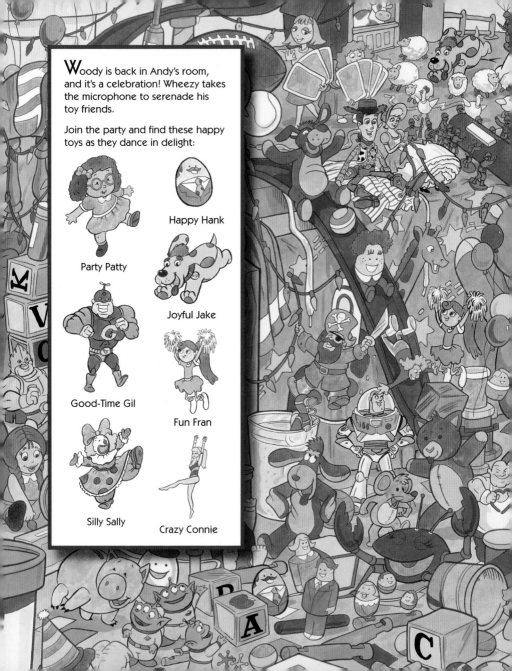

Woody is back in Andy's room, and it's a celebration! Wheezy takes the microphone to serenade his toy friends.

Join the party and find these happy toys as they dance in delight:

Party Patty

Happy Hank

Joyful Jake

Good-Time Gil

Fun Fran

Silly Sally

Crazy Connie

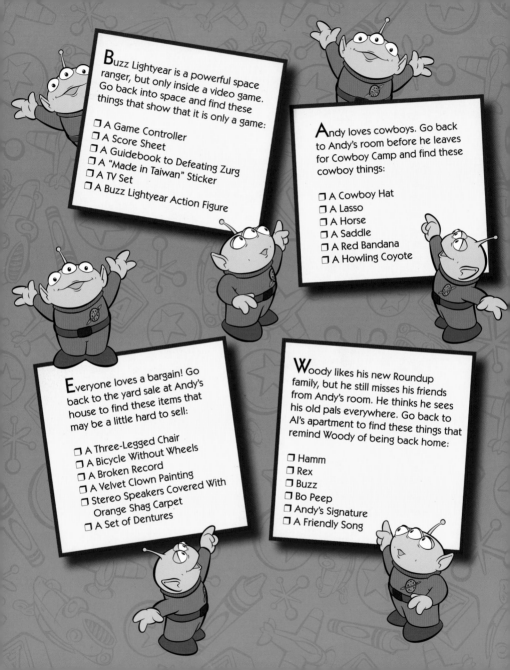

Buzz Lightyear is a powerful space ranger, but only inside a video game. Go back into space and find these things that show that it is only a game:

☐ A Game Controller
☐ A Score Sheet
☐ A Guidebook to Defeating Zurg
☐ A "Made in Taiwan" Sticker
☐ A TV Set
☐ A Buzz Lightyear Action Figure

Andy loves cowboys. Go back to Andy's room before he leaves for Cowboy Camp and find these cowboy things:

☐ A Cowboy Hat
☐ A Lasso
☐ A Horse
☐ A Saddle
☐ A Red Bandana
☐ A Howling Coyote

Everyone loves a bargain! Go back to the yard sale at Andy's house to find these items that may be a little hard to sell:

☐ A Three-Legged Chair
☐ A Bicycle Without Wheels
☐ A Broken Record
☐ A Velvet Clown Painting
☐ Stereo Speakers Covered With Orange Shag Carpet
☐ A Set of Dentures

Woody likes his new Roundup family, but he still misses his friends from Andy's room. He thinks he sees his old pals everywhere. Go back to Al's apartment to find these things that remind Woody of being back home:

☐ Hamm
☐ Rex
☐ Buzz
☐ Bo Peep
☐ Andy's Signature
☐ A Friendly Song

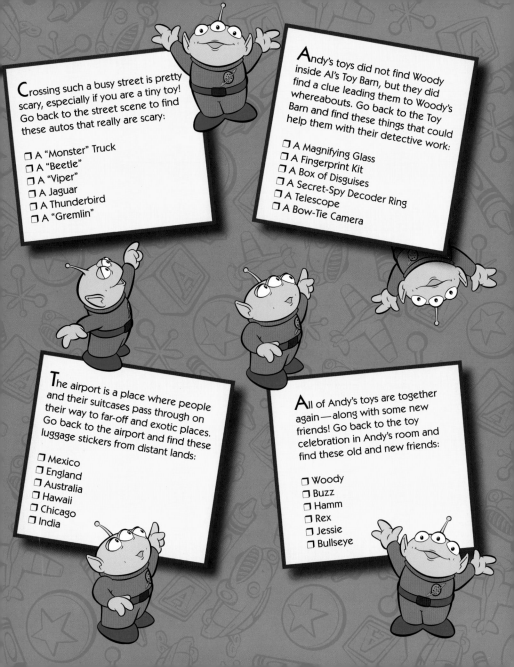

Crossing such a busy street is pretty scary, especially if you are a tiny toy! Go back to the street scene to find these autos that really are scary:

- ☐ A "Monster" Truck
- ☐ A "Beetle"
- ☐ A "Viper"
- ☐ A Jaguar
- ☐ A Thunderbird
- ☐ A "Gremlin"

Andy's toys did not find Woody inside Al's Toy Barn, but they did find a clue leading them to Woody's whereabouts. Go back to the Toy Barn and find these things that could help them with their detective work:

- ☐ A Magnifying Glass
- ☐ A Fingerprint Kit
- ☐ A Box of Disguises
- ☐ A Secret-Spy Decoder Ring
- ☐ A Telescope
- ☐ A Bow-Tie Camera

The airport is a place where people and their suitcases pass through on their way to far-off and exotic places. Go back to the airport and find these luggage stickers from distant lands:

- ☐ Mexico
- ☐ England
- ☐ Australia
- ☐ Hawaii
- ☐ Chicago
- ☐ India

All of Andy's toys are together again—along with some new friends! Go back to the toy celebration in Andy's room and find these old and new friends:

- ☐ Woody
- ☐ Buzz
- ☐ Hamm
- ☐ Rex
- ☐ Jessie
- ☐ Bullseye